Author: Ashley Madden
Illustrator: Chariz Elaine

support@dottiedotts.com

DOTTIE LOVES TO SWIM.

She would stay in the pool
all day if she could.

She can swim from
one end of the pool
to the other.

She can dive into
the deep end.

She can even do a backflip in the water!

**BUT DOTTIE
HAS A PROBLEM.**

She is embarrassed
that she likes to swim.

One day, Dottie's friend
Andy invited her over for a
POOL PARTY.

"I DON'T THINK
I CAN GO,"
said Dottie.

"Why?"
Andy asked.

"Cats aren't supposed to like water. **I'LL LOOK SILLY,**" Dottie answered.

"IT WILL BE OKAY."
"We're all your friends,"
Andy said.

Dottie thought about it for a few days. She decided Andy was right.

Dottie called Andy and told her that she would go to the party.

The day of the party finally came. Dottie felt

NERVOUS.

All her friends were in the water, but Dottie just sat by the pool.

"THEY MIGHT MAKE FUN OF ME," Dottie replied.

"Okay, I'll put on
my swimsuit,"
said Dottie.

Dottie told herself to be
BRAVE
and walked into the pool.

Dottie swam over to Andy.
NO ONE STARED AT HER.

Everyone splashed and played for the rest of the day.

Dottie's friends were glad to have her in the pool.

THEY LIKE HER AS SHE IS.

Ashley Madden lives in Florida with her husband, her two daughters, and her labradoodle, Tinkerbell. ("Tink," for short.) She also has three cats: Sabbie, Juna, and Brooks. The friendship that her dog and cats share is part of what inspired her to create Dottie the cat and her dog friend, Andy. Ashley believes that kids learn the most and build strong characters while they are having fun, and she hopes they will have fun reading about Dottie!

ABOUT THE ILLUSTRATOR

Chariz Elaine is a cat lover whose dream is to become an illustrator since she was seven. She pursued her career as a graphic designer while still pursuing her dream to become an illustrator. She loves doing illustrations for children's books as it calms her, and loves to see every child's joy who sees her colorful drawings.

More fun books about
DOTTIE DOTTS

also available at
amazon.com
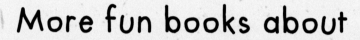

mybook.to/dottiedottsbooks

DOTTIE DOTTS
ART CLASS

WRITTEN BY
ASHLEY MADDEN
ILLUSTRATED BY
CHARIZ ELAINE

DOTTIE DOTTS
BAKE SALE

WRITTEN BY
ASHLEY MADDEN
ILLUSTRATED BY
CHARIZ ELAINE

DOTTIE DOTTS
HOP SCOTCH

WRITTEN BY
ASHLEY MADDEN
ILLUSTRATED BY
CHARIZ ELAINE

DOTTIE DOTTS
MOMMY'S MAKEUP

STORY BY
ASHLEY MADDEN
ILLUSTRATIONS BY
JERIC TAN

Made in the USA
Columbia, SC
16 March 2021